Star Sisters
and the
Big Show

Written by Jennifer Blecher

Illustrated by Anne Zimanski

Disclaimer: This is a work of fiction. Some characters within it are based on living persons. However, all actions, statements, and thoughts attributed to such characters, and all other events and incidents depicted in this work, are either the products of the author's imagination or are used in a fictitious manner.

TO OLIVIA – FOR LIGHTING UP MY LIFE.

Prologue

One thousand years ago, a mighty river flowed through the ancient land of Illustria. Past fields of wildflowers and through lush green valleys, the river charted its winding course. Like all good rivers, it quenched people's thirst and sustained the earth. But the river of Illustria did not flow with water alone, it also flowed with magic. This river had the power to heal.

The royal family of Illustria was kind and they invited the sick, the weak, and the needy to drink from the river's shores.

From far and wide people came and, sip by sip, they were healed.

Until one day an evil Queen invaded Illustria, hoping to claim the river's powers for her own. Though she was able to defeat the royal family of Illustria and banish them from the land, she was not able to control the river. Sensing that there was no kindness in the evil Queen's soul, the river shrank, its roaring waters becoming a trickling stream. Everyone thought the river's magic was gone forever. But everyone was wrong.

For before the evil Queen invaded, the King of Illustria gave his daughters, the princess sisters, necklaces made from star-shaped emeralds that were unearthed from the shores of the river. These necklaces gave the princesses the power to vanish and magically travel to far away lands where they would help spread kindness. The kingdom of Illustria is no more, but the necklaces have survived. And their magic lives on.

It lives around the necks of two regular girls named Coco and Lucy. New to their town and both a little lonely, Coco and Lucy met when they fell into the stream that was once Illustria's mighty river. Each girl was wearing one of the princesses' necklaces, only the emerald stars were now stone stars.

A tiny fairy named Grissella, a lone survivor

from the days of Illustria, popped out of a

tree trunk to help Coco and Lucy understand that they had been brought together not by chance, but by fate. By magic. Of all the girls in the world, they had been chosen to carry on the mission of the royal family of Illustria: to spread kindness.

Though Coco and Lucy had their doubts, when they said a special chant the stone stars on their necklaces turned to glowing emerald stars and they were whisked away on a magical kindness spreading adventure. They don't know when the magic will come again, or where they'll be taken, but they know it will happen. For they are the Star Sisters. And they are ready!

Chapter One

The sun beat down on the ice cream

cones. *Drip. Drip. Drip.* Coco and Lucy

twirled the cones in their hands, trying their

best to keep pace with the melting streams

of strawberry and vanilla. These were the

kinds of ice cream cones that required lots of twirling experience.

"Delicious," said Coco as she licked the strawberry cone.

"Scrum-diddily-umptious," said Lucy as she licked the vanilla cone.

"And when we're done eating we can just rinse our hands off in the pool," said Coco.

"Yep," said Lucy. "No soap needed!"

Ah, summer. Land of sticky fingers, swimming pools, and flip-flops. Of sand between toes and warm ocean breezes. A time for popsicles, sidewalk chalk, and fireflies at night. It was Coco and Lucy's favorite season. Especially this year, because this year they had each other.

As soon as they finished their ice cream cones, they rushed over to the side of the local swimming pool, held hands, and counted down: three, two, one – *cannonball!* With a giant splash, Coco and Lucy sank underwater, giggling as tiny air bubbles tickled the inside of their noses. They were just about to begin playing mermaid sisters, a game about friendly mermaids and scary enemy sharks, when a loud whistle blew. "Adult swim," yelled a lifeguard wearing a red bathing suit. "All kids out of the water."

"But we can't get out of the water," said Coco to the lifeguard. "We're mermaids."

"Our tails will shrivel up on dry land," explained Lucy.

"Sorry," said the lifeguard. "All kids out of the pool, mermaid kids included. It's the rule."

"But adults don't even like to play mermaid sisters," said Lucy as she climbed out of the pool.

"All they do is swim in straight lines," agreed Coco. "What's the point of that?"

Coco and Lucy found their towels and lay down on the grass by the side of the pool. A gentle wind blew over their wet backs as Coco pulled a stray dandelion from the ground. Holding the fuzzy stem, she began to remove the yellow petals one by one.

"Magic," said Coco as she pulled off the first petal. "Magic not," she continued as she pulled off the second petal.

Coco repeated this pattern — magic, magic not— until there was just one petal left. "Magic!" exclaimed Coco as the last petal fell to the ground. "It landed on magic!"

"Oh, I hope that dandelion's right," said Lucy. "We've been waiting *forever* for our next magical adventure."

"And ever and ever and ever," agreed Coco with a sigh.

Chapter Two

To be honest, Coco and Lucy hadn't really been waiting forever. But they had been waiting long enough for school to end and summer to start. Their backpacks were zipped up tight and their heavy winter coats

stuffed in the very back of their closets. The
thick boots that made their feet sweat and
rubbed in all the wrong places were swapped
for sandals as light as air or, better yet, no
shoes at all.

Most importantly, the school year rhythm
of hallway bells and circle time on the rug

was replaced with long days at the swimming pool and lots of free time together.

Which is just the way Coco and Lucy liked it. They loved playing mermaid sisters and kicking under the water while holding hands. They could spend hours practicing their handstands in the shallow end of the pool. (Coco always got water up her nose, which made her sneeze. *Achoo!*)

Even saying good-bye at the end of the day, the backs of their t-shirts wet from their dripping hair and their bodies tired from all the swimming, wasn't all that bad because they knew they would be meeting up bright and early the next day. And who knew what the next summer day would bring, perhaps the magical adventure they were hoping for?

Speaking of magical adventures, as Coco and Lucy continued pulling the petals off more dandelions, the gentle wind that had been blowing turned stronger and the sky grew dark. The loose petals blew off the grass and into the pool that was now spotted with tiny waves.

Coco and Lucy rolled off their stomachs and sat up. Strangely, the pool area had emptied. All the chairs were pushed in and the umbrellas were closed. The only sign of movement was from a squirrel that raced across the cement, paused to wiggle its nose

in the air, and then scampered away.

"Where'd everybody go?" asked Lucy.

"Beats me," said Coco with a shrug. "But this feels kind of familiar."

"Good familiar?" asked Lucy.

"Great familiar," said Coco. "I think it might be time for our necklaces to shine like emeralds again."

"Oh, I hope so," said Lucy. "Let's try."

So Coco and Lucy joined hands, and the moment their fingers touched they knew without a doubt that another magical journey was about to begin. It was as if electric sparks bounced between their bodies. They smiled and said their special chant:

Star sisters, friends forever.

Through thick and thin, we're both in.

And sure enough, the stars on their necklaces started to glow. Like an ocean wave washing over the sand, the stone stars slowly changed into brilliant green emerald stars. The light from the emeralds combined and started to circle around the two girls, creating a halo of bright sparkles. One rumble later, Coco and Lucy were still in their bathing suits next to a swimming pool. But it was not the same swimming pool. Not even close.

Chapter Three

"Wow," said Coco, looking around at the new egg-shaped swimming pool and the enormous white house with black shutters that stood behind it. "Fancy."

"Smell the air," said Lucy. "It smells like sunshine and flowers and..."

"Cupcakes," interrupted Coco. "Look!"

Coco pointed to a girl sitting at the edge of the pool, her bare feet dangling in the water. Next to the girl was a plate with two cupcakes that were topped with fluffy pink frosting and loads of rainbow sprinkles. Slowly, the girl started to strum the guitar she was holding in her lap.

"She looks so sad," said Lucy as the girl pushed a strand of curly blond hair out of her eyes. "Who could be sad sitting next to beautiful cupcakes like those?"

"Beats me," said Coco. "If only I were closer I would..."

Coco pretended to reach out and grab a cupcake, but at that exact moment a black cat jumped down from a tree and landed with a loud screech. Coco was so startled that she lost her balance and fell into the swimming pool. Lucy didn't know what to do, but she knew that she and Coco needed to stay together, so she jumped into the pool as well.

"Oh my!" said the girl with the guitar as Coco and Lucy hit the water with loud splashes. "Who are you?"

Now, Coco and Lucy were two very smart girls. They both loved to read books, work on math problems, and do complicated puzzles with teeny tiny pieces. Lucy was even learning how to play chess. But in that moment, in the deep end of a strange swimming pool, in front of a strange girl, with water dripping in their eyes and down the tips of their noses, Coco and Lucy were speechless. So they did what their parents always told them to do: tell the truth.

"I'm Coco," said Coco as she swam to the stairs of the pool.

"And I'm Lucy," said Lucy as she followed Coco out of the water.

"Oh! Great!" said the girl, smiling wide. "You must be the new neighbors! My mom said two girls my age were moving in next door and I saw the moving truck pull up this morning. I'm so glad you came over  in your bathing suits. And those are super cool necklaces."

Coco and Lucy touched the emerald stars on their necklaces. The emeralds were glowing bright, a sure sign that a Star Sisters adventure was underway. It seemed that this time they were acting as new neighbors. Well, that didn't sound so bad. After all, it would be great to live next door to a friend with her own swimming pool. Especially when that friend also had the most delicious looking cupcakes.

"I'm Trina," said the girl. "Trina Fast. Wait here and I'll change into my bathing suit." Trina carefully laid down her guitar and raced into the large house. She came back a few minutes later wearing a glittery red bathing suit.

Now, there's something about a pool of water on a hot summer day that just makes everything okay. Even though Coco and Lucy didn't know where they were or what they had been sent to do, for the moment they forgot about all that and had a great time swimming with Trina. They taught her all the rules of mermaid sisters and it turned out that Trina had a great mermaid kick. As the sun began to sink in the sky, the three girls climbed out of the pool and lay down on fresh fluffy towels.

Chapter Four

All was quiet and well until — *rumble, rumble, rumble* — a strange growling noise rose from Lucy's belly. Quite some time had passed since Lucy finished the melting vanilla ice cream cone at the local pool and she had been doing a lot of swimming. Lucy was hungry! And, to make matters worse, the plate of cupcakes was still out on the table, sending the tempting smell of sugar, cake, and sprinkles right under Lucy's nose! Finally, poor Lucy couldn't wait any longer.

"Trina, are you going to eat those cupcakes?" she asked. "Because if you don't want to, I definitely will."

Trina jumped up from her towel and leaned over the plate of cupcakes, as if to protect them from a pack of hungry animals. "No!" she said. "You can't eat these cupcakes. I'm saving them for someone else."

"Oh," said Lucy, feeling a little
embarrassed although she wasn't quite sure
why. "Sorry. I didn't realize."

Trina shook her head slowly. "No, I'm sorry," she said. "I know the cupcakes have been sitting here all afternoon. But before you guys came I was waiting for someone. Someone really important." Trina's shoulders drooped and she picked up her guitar.

Sometimes, on their missions as Star Sisters, it took Coco and Lucy quite a while to figure out what they were supposed to do to help spread kindness. But this time, seeing Trina in her sparkly red bathing suit moping with her guitar, they knew right away that she was the one they were sent to help. Coco and Lucy weren't sure exactly what they were supposed to do, but they thought the cupcakes might be a clue.

"Who *are* the cupcakes for?" asked Coco.

"Oh, they're for Lake," said Trina with a sigh. "She's my friend from summer camp. It's been the best summer ever. I've been going to this camp for kids who like to perform on stage. I'm going to be a famous

singer when I grow up. Lake wants to be a

dancer. The ballerina kind. We met on the

first day of camp because we both ran

straight to the top of the double slide at first

recess. We almost knocked each other

over!"

"We've been friends ever since," continued Trina. "And every day after camp Lake comes over to my house and we eat cupcakes and practice what we learned. I play my guitar and Lake dances. But I guess she's not coming over today."

"Why not?" asked Lucy.

"I don't know," said Trina. "Lake and I are supposed to do a performance together at the end of summer talent show tomorrow. I'm going to sing a song I wrote and Lake is going to dance to it. But this afternoon I was backstage practicing my song and I saw Lake run out of the theater. She missed our rehearsal slot. When I went to go find her,

Lake was gone. I thought she'd come over this afternoon like always, but it's almost dinnertime. I guess she's not coming."

Before Coco and Lucy could ask any more questions, Trina's mom opened the door and yelled, "Din-ner! Time to come inside!"

"Hey, you guys want to have a sleepover?" asked Trina. "You can sleep in my room. I have a big bed with a canopy on top."

"Really?" said Lucy. She had seen a picture of a canopy bed in a magazine once and she'd been thinking about it ever since. The bed was so beautiful, like a delicate white tent that could catch all your lovely dreams and save them forever. She'd wanted to sleep in one ever since.

Plus, she and Coco didn't exactly have anywhere else to sleep. Or anything to wear to sleep. Or any clothes at all!

"And I've got lots of clothes you guys can borrow," said Trina as if reading Lucy's mind. "After all, your stuff is probably still in boxes from the move."

Coco and Lucy smiled. Problem solved. Phew.

Chapter Five

After dinner, Coco and Lucy followed

Trina to her bedroom. It was stunning, with

light pink walls, curtains decorated with tiny

rosebuds, and a crystal chandelier hanging

from the ceiling. As promised, an enormous

canopy bed piled high with ruffled and lace

pillows occupied the center of the room.

Trina opened the double doors to her closet.

"Choose any clothes you like," she said.

Coco and Lucy each changed into a

comfy pair of soft pajamas and climbed onto

the canopy bed. Lucy smiled. The bed was

just as wonderful as she'd imagined. It was definitely a great place to spend the night.

"You guys want to hear a song?" asked Trina.

"Yes," said Coco and Lucy at the same time. Which they followed immediately with, "Jinx!" And then, "Jinx again!" just to be safe. Giggling, they sat crisscross applesauce on the bed as Trina tuned her guitar.

"Okay," she said. "Here's the song I'm going to sing at tomorrow's camp talent show. It's called, *We Are Never Going Down The Slide Together.*"

Trina played a few introductory notes on her guitar and then started to sing:

Do you remember when, we were on the slide,
And you said you'd never leave my side.
But then you went too fast,
And I said this friendship will never last.
You like to dance and I like to sing,
So this will be our final slide till next spring.

Because we are never ever ever, going down the slide together.

No we are never ever ever, going down the slide together.

Trina smiled and looked up. "What do you guys think?" she asked.

Coco and Lucy weren't sure what to say. On one hand, the song was actually pretty great. Trina's voice was soft, yet strong, and she sang each word with such emotion that Coco and Lucy felt like they were right there on the playground racing down a slide along with Trina.

But on the other hand, the words were rather sad. They left Coco and Lucy wondering what happened to the friend on the slide? Did they have a fight? Did they lose touch? Did they...

"Wait a second," said Lucy. "Did you say this is the song that you're going to sing at the camp talent show tomorrow? The one that you practiced today at the dress rehearsal? The song Lake was going to dance along to?"

"Yep," said Trina. "I think it's my best work so far. I mean, unless you guys don't like it. You look a little surprised. Did I hit some bad notes? Do you think the beat's too slow for dancing? Maybe that's why Lake rushed out?"

Coco and Lucy looked at each other with an are-you-thinking-what-I'm-thinking kind of face. When each girl nodded they knew that yes, they were both thinking the same thing.

"Well," said Coco slowly. "Your singing was great and the beat sounds fine, but I think we may know why Lake didn't come over this afternoon for cupcakes."

"Why?" asked Trina.

"You said earlier that Lake heard you sing this song backstage and then she rushed out, right?" said Lucy.

"Yep," said Trina.

"And you also said that Lake is a friend who likes to dance and you like to sing," said Coco.

"She's more than a friend," said Trina. "She's like a sister to me." Trina's voice trailed off.

"Trina, Lake probably thinks the song is about *her*," said Lucy. "That's probably why she ran out of the theater and why she hasn't come over since. I think you hurt

Lake's feelings."

Chapter Six

Trina looked stunned. Shocked.

Confused. She put her guitar down and

shook her head. "But that doesn't make any

sense," she said. "All summer long my

counselors have been telling me to write

songs about what I'm feeling, about what's in my heart. That's all I did. There's a double slide on the playground at camp and Lake and I love to do slide races at free time. It's one of those slides where your bum lifts off at the very end and, for just one second, you fly through the air like a bird."

"All I did was write about that," Trina continued. "About how I'm sad that we won't be able to do slide races again until next summer when school ends and we go back to camp."

"But that's not all you wrote in your song," said Coco. "Didn't you write something about the friendship not lasting?"

Trina picked up her guitar and sang the two lines that Coco was talking about:

But then you went too fast, and I said this friendship will never last.

"That line?" asked Trina. "But I didn't really mean the friendship would never last. Lake and I are going to be friends forever. I just needed to make the song dramatic. You know, so people would hear the song and remember it forever. But I guess I was only thinking about the people in the audience, all their faces looking up at me on stage while I sing. I wasn't thinking about the one person who really matters. I wasn't thinking about Lake at all."

Trina's bottom lip started to quiver and she felt like her belly was twisting in a giant knot. "Poor Lake," she said as tears started to drip down her cheeks and land on her guitar. "I must have really hurt her feelings. What do I do now?"

Even though it was terrible to see Trina so upset, both Coco and Lucy smiled a little bit. There were many things that Coco and

Lucy couldn't do. They couldn't pour their

own milk without spilling, or reach the

cookies that their moms kept on the tippy

top shelf, and sometimes Coco had trouble

tying the laces on her sneakers.

But they were Star Sisters. And if there was one thing that Star Sisters were really good at, it was spreading kindness and fixing friendship problems.

"Don't worry," said Lucy as she gave Trina a hug. "We'll help you figure it out."

Chapter Seven

And so a plan was born. With Coco and Lucy's help, Trina decided to write a new song to perform at the camp talent show the next morning – a song that came from her heart and expressed her feelings, but also considered the feelings of her friend.

It turns out, writing a brand new song wasn't so easy. There was the music, which consisted of notes and chords, and then there were the words, which were broken into sections called chorus and verse.

As the moon shone bright in the night sky and Trina's mom warned them once  again that it was five minutes until lights out, Coco, Lucy, and Trina decided they didn't have enough time to write a whole new song. They would stick with the general slide idea but focus on writing new words.

"But it has to ring true," Trina reminded them. "It has to be real."

"Okay," said Lucy, not entirely sure what Trina was talking about, but figuring she'd give it a shot anyways. "How about, *Then you hit the ground, And you were upside down.*"

"Not quite right," said Trina, shaking her head.

"I got it!" exclaimed Coco. "How about, *Then I saw your underwear, And it had a picture of a pink teddy bear.*"

Trina and Lucy laughed. "Funny," said Trina. "But still not the right message."

"Good point," said Coco.

Then Trina closed her eyes and started playing notes on her guitar. She hummed softly, until suddenly, Trina opened her eyes and smiled. "How about this," she said.

Do you remember when, we were on the slide,
And you said you'd never leave my side.
And so I reached for your hand,
Because I knew you would understand.

You like to dance and I like to sing,
But together we can do anything.

Because we will always, always, go down the slide together.

Yes we will always, always, go down the slide together.

"It's perfect," said Coco as she clapped her hands.

"As perfect as the most delicious cupcake with loads of rainbow sprinkles on top," agreed Lucy.

"Thanks, guys," said Trina. "I like it a lot."

The girls cuddled up together in Trina's canopy bed. It was way, way, *way* past their bedtime, but they were so excited that they had a hard time falling asleep. Eventually, as Trina quietly hummed the new words of her friendship song, the three girls felt their eyelids grow heavy and they fell asleep.

The next morning was not quite so peaceful. The sun had barely risen in the sky when a bird that was perched on the windowsill outside of Trina's room decided to sing its own loud song — *cucaw!, cucaw!, cucaw!* The three girls covered their ears.

"Make it stop," groaned Trina.

"Please," moaned Coco.

"With a cherry on top," begged Lucy.

But, like a baby who wants out from her crib, there was no stopping the cries of this morning bird. Slowly, as light seeped in through the rosebud curtains, the girls peeled their eyes open. Then Trina sat straight up.

"I just remembered, it's talent show day," she said. "Come on sleepy heads, rise and shine. I can't wait for Lake to hear the new song."

What followed was a transformation worthy of Cinderella's fairy godmother.

With a bibbidi, bobbidi, boo, Trina changed from a tired girl with curly hair flying every which way to a focused performer.

Off went her ruffled pink nightgown and on went her jean skirt, red t-shirt and red cowboy boots. Her blond curls were tamed with water and wrapped in a flowered headband. "My signature look," she explained. "Every singer has to have one."

By the time her mom called, "Trina! Coco! Lucy! I made chocolate chip pancakes for breakfast," Trina was ready for action.

Chapter Eight

"Wow," said Coco when she saw the camp auditorium for the very first time. "This is way scarier than I thought it would be. This place is huge."

"It feels like a gazillion tiny flashlights are pointing right at us," said Lucy as she shielded her eyes from the spotlights.

"And it's a long way down," said Coco.

The girls peered over the edge of the stage where that day's talent show was taking place. It wasn't like their stage at school, which was really just a wooden platform a tiny bit higher than the gymnasium floor. This stage was raised well off the ground, with lots of beeping equipment and velvet curtains marking off all the backstage happenings.

"Trina must be really brave to get up here and perform all by herself," said Lucy.

"Not all by herself," said Coco. "Lake
will be here too."

"I sure hope so," said Lucy. "Everything's
better with a friend."

For just one moment, Coco and Lucy
forgot about Trina and Lake and thought
about themselves. Which was
understandable because it was only a short

time ago that Coco and Lucy were all alone. Maybe each girl would have had the courage to go on these magical adventures, her emerald star shining, without the other girl, but they were glad they wouldn't have to find that out.

Because sometimes a friend is more than just someone to play mermaid sisters with in the swimming pool. Sometimes a friend is the person who fills your heart with all the things that hearts need: like love, courage, and a lot of reasons to giggle.

Which brings us back to Trina and Lake, because at that moment, there was no giggling going on. None at all.

"Coco! Lucy!" called Trina frantically. "I can't find Lake anywhere! She should be backstage stretching with the other dancers. The talent show starts in one hour!"

"Oh no!" said Lucy. "Are you sure? Did you look everywhere?"

"All over the theater," said Trina. "Even the secret spot in the wardrobe room where we sometimes go to play dress-up with the costumes. I don't know what to do! I have to stay here or else I'll miss my slot in the show. *Our* slot in the show."

"Okay," said Coco. "You stay here. Lucy and I will go look for Lake."

"Please hurry!" said Trina. "This is the final talent show of the summer. We've been practicing for weeks. I don't want Lake to miss it because I hurt her feelings."

Chapter Nine

Coco and Lucy left the theater and
started walking around the rest of the
building calling Lake's name. In and out of
bathrooms, down hallways, and into

classrooms they went, all with no sign of Lake. "She's disappeared into thin air," said Coco.

"We can't give up," said Lucy. "Lake has to be here somewhere."

"But where?" said Coco. "We've searched the entire place." Coco sighed and walked over to a large row of windows that looked out onto the parking lot behind the building. And there, off in the distance behind the minivans, cars, and bikes, she saw a playground. A playground with a double slide.

"Lucy, look!" she said. "That must be the slide that Trina was talking about. The one she and Lake like to play on. The slide where they met for the first time. Maybe that's where Lake is hiding."

"It's worth a shot," said Lucy. "Let's go."

Coco and Lucy raced out of the building and down to the playground. Sure enough, huddled all alone in the shadow of the green plastic slide, was a girl their age.

"Lake?" asked Coco. "Is that you?"

"Who are you?" said Lake. "How do you know my name?"

"We're Trina's friends," said Lucy. "She sent us to find you."

"Why?" asked Lake with a sigh. "Did she write another song about me."

"Actually, yes," said Coco. "But it's not what you think. Trina feels badly about the original song. She never meant to hurt your feelings and she wants to make things better. She wants to perform with you at the talent show today."

"Sorry, guys," said Lake. "But I don't want to perform with her. Dancing is my favorite thing in the world. When I'm up there on the stage, I just feel so free." Lake bent her arms as if they were blowing in the breeze and, with that one slight movement, Coco and Lucy could tell she was a great dancer.

"But Trina's song, it just made me so sad," continued Lake. "The words...they were just...not nice. They hurt my feelings. I can't dance when I'm sad."

"Lake, please," begged Lucy. "Just give Trina one chance to fix her mistake. She told us all about your summer, about what close friends you are and how you would play together every afternoon after camp."

"And yesterday when you didn't come over she was so upset," said Coco. "She wouldn't let anyone eat your cupcake. She

just left it all alone on the plate. Not a single sprinkle was touched, not even the pink ones."

"Really?" said Lake. "She did that?"

"Yep," said Coco. "And she also wrote a really great new song. One that came straight from her heart."

Lake looked at the sneakers on her feet. "Even if I did want to dance at the talent show, I don't have anything to wear. I was so upset this morning that I left my ballet bag in the trunk of my mom's car by accident."

"Well, then," said Lucy. "We're going to have to make a quick pit stop. I hear you know where the wardrobe room is."

Chapter Ten

Coco, Lucy, and Lake dug through piles of frilly costumes until they found a dance outfit and ballet slippers that fit Lake. They raced back to the theater and arrived backstage with no time to spare.

"Next up on stage," said an announcer, "we are pleased to welcome a very talented duo: Trina on the guitar and Lake dancing ballet."

From behind the curtains Coco and Lucy could see Trina walking onto the stage all alone. She looked nervous and unsure of herself, very different from the girl who'd zipped up her cowboy boots with a big smile just a few hours before. She moved slowly, as if she was trying to find her way through a complicated maze.

But then Lake tapped her on the shoulder and it was as if Trina had been sprinkled with fairy dust. She seemed instantly lighter, like she could take off into the sky at a moments notice. Holding hands, the girls took their places on stage.

"Phew," whispered Coco. "That was close."

The lights dimmed and Trina closed her eyes. She placed her fingers on the strings of her guitar and began to strum. As the sound of her guitar grew in strength, so did

Lake's body. Across the stage Lake glided

and leapt and twirled as Trina sang the new

words:

> Do you remember when we were on the slide,
> And you said you'd never leave my side.
> And so I reached for your hand,
> Because I knew you would understand.

> You like to dance and I like to sing,
> But together we can do anything.

> Because we will always, always, go down the
> slide together.

> Yes we will always, always, go down the slide
> together.

When the song ended Trina and Lake
gave each other a big hug. They walked off
the stage hand-in-hand.

"Great dancing," said Trina.

"Great song," said Lake.

"I'm sorry about the old one," said Trina. "I got caught up in what rhymed and what I thought people would want to hear and I forgot about your feelings. I made a really big mistake."

"That's okay," said Lake. "Everyone makes mistakes. At least you saved my cupcake."

"What?" asked Trina, confused.

"Coco and Lucy," said Lake. "They told me about the cupcake at your pool. How you left it out all afternoon for me. Now that's a true friend."

Trina laughed. "One last slide race before the summer ends?"

"Definitely," said Lake.

As Trina and Lake ran off towards the playground, Coco and Lucy smiled. They had saved a friendship and spread kindness.

Their work as Star Sisters was done.

"Time to go home," said Lucy.

"Yep," said Coco. "It's time."

They took one last look at the stage where a friendship had almost ended. But it hadn't, thanks to them. A ray of light from an overhead spotlight caught the emerald star hanging on Coco's neck, sending specks of green into the air.

Coco and Lucy found a quiet spot behind the curtains, held hands, and said their favorite words:

Star sisters, friends forever.

Through thick and thin, we're both in.

A flash and a blink later, they were back at their local swimming pool on that hot summer day. The emerald stars on their necklaces turned back to stones but they didn't mind. Coco and Lucy knew the stars would be shining bright again in no time.

THE END

Can't get enough of the Star Sisters? You're in luck. See what else Coco and Lucy are up to...

It's the night before the royal wedding and all is not well in Luckingham Palace. When Princess-to-be Caroline and her sister Poppy have a fight over Poppy's wedding attire, both sisters feel their friendship being tested. Will the event the world has been waiting for be ruined? Not with the Star Sisters on the job!

Join Coco and Lucy as they save the day with the help of a friendly seamstress, some creative thinking, and a big helping of sisterly love.

www.star-sisters.com

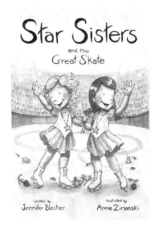

Figure skaters Nina Kerrington and Tara Harling have dreamed of going to the Olympics since they laced up their first pair of ice skates. But when Nina falls and hurts her knee the day before the qualifying competition, it turns out that her slip was more than just an accident.

Get ready as Coco and Lucy take to the ice to help a little girl learn a whole lot about sportsmanship, kindness, and the importance of saying "I'm sorry".

www.star-sisters.com

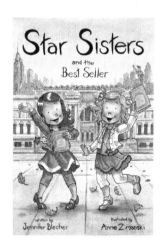

K.J. Dowling has big dreams of writing a book. But when no one takes her seriously, K.J. starts to doubt herself. It's Coco and Lucy to the rescue in an urban adventure in the city where dreams come true – NYC.

Join the girls as they make their way through the Metropolitan Museum of Art, around Central Park, and down 5th Avenue to show one special little girl that being different is a good thing and believing in yourself is even better. An inspiring read for everyone with big dreams.

www.star-sisters.com

Visit **www.star-sisters.com** for coloring pages, craft activities, and all the latest info on where Coco and Lucy are popping up next.

Westgate Publishing

Made in the USA
Lexington, KY
02 December 2016